D0801465

To

Lucy,

Merry Christmas!

Love from

Grammy & Pop Pop

2020

Lucy sees a present
wrapped up neatly with a bow.
The label says her name,
and the wrapping seems to glow.

"This present is for me!" cries Lucy,
with the biggest grin.
She opens it to look inside,
and suddenly falls in!

Lucy's in the frosty woods.
She can't believe her eyes.
To find a world inside a box
is such a big surprise!

ELF WORKSHOP

NORTH POLE EXPRESS

SANTA'S HOUSE

She stares up at a signpost
to see which way to go.
"Santa's house?" she says in awe,
then runs through sparkly snow.

Lucy spots a village
and a family up ahead.
When she gets close she gasps because
they're made of gingerbread!

The daddy smiles at Lucy.
"You want Santa's house, I guess?
You'll get there so much quicker
on the ol' North Pole Express."

NORTH POLE EXPRESS

SANTA'S HOUSE

Lucy's at the station
when she spots a little elf.
The elf tells her, "I'm off to see
Santa Claus, himself."

Lucy is excited.
"Yes, I'm off to see him too!
But I'm not sure which way to go.
Can I come along with you?"

They hear a distant chugging sound,
then see the train appear.
The elf says, "Lucy, this is it!
The North Pole Express is here!"

ALL ABOARD,
LUCY

A small penguin conductor
brings the steam train to a stop.
"All aboard!" he shouts to Lucy.
"Come ride with me up top."

Lucy has the perfect seat
and an even better view.
Snowy forests whiz by her,
while the chimney toots

"choo-choo!"

No

They reach their destination.
Lucy's face is full of cheer.
The penguin blows his whistle,
shouting, "Hooray! We are here!"

The elf takes Lucy to a house.
Mrs. Claus greets her with glee.
"I'm so glad you are here at last.
Come in and sit with me!"

Lucy sips hot chocolate,
and eats warm cookies from a plate.
The elf says, "Lucy, we must go.
We really can't be late."

Lucy is led through
a busy workshop full of elves,
where a million shiny toys
sit high on countless shelves.

"Will I see Santa?" Lucy hopes.
"I think that would be neat."
The elf says, "Yes! That's why you're here.
He really wants to meet!"

"Ho ho hello, Lucy!
You've been sooo good this year.
That's why I left a magic gift—
so I could bring you here!"

to Lucy

"Yes, you wished to meet me.
I made that wish come true.
And now, I have a special toy.
One I made…just for you."

Lucy peeks inside the box,
then quickly lifts her head.
She no longer sees Santa—
but is back at home instead!

Her trip has been amazing,
a night she won't forget.
And in the box is Santa's gift:
a North Pole Express train set!

Lucy, hop on board the
NORTH POLE EXPRESS!

Draw yourself and your friends
on the train to see Santa.

Written by J.D. Green
Designed by Jane Gollner

Copyright © Orangutan Books Ltd. 2020

Put Me In The Story is a
registered trademark of Sourcebooks, Inc.
All rights reserved.

Published by Put Me In The Story,
a publication of Sourcebooks, Inc.
P.O. Box 4410, Naperville, Illinois 60567-4410
(630) 536-1104
www.putmeinthestory.com

Date of Production: July 2020
Run Number: 5018824
Printed and bound in China (GD)
10 9 8 7 6 5 4 3 2

MIX
Paper from
responsible sources
FSC® C117745

Bestselling books starring your child!
www.putmeinthestory.com